ON THE LINE

FRED BOWEN

PEACHTREE
ATLANTA

Published by
PEACHTREE PUBLISHERS
1700 Chattahoochee Avenue
Atlanta, Georgia 30318-2112

www.peachtree-online.com

Cover design by Thomas Gonzalez and Maureen Withee
Book design by Melanie McMahon Ives and Loraine M. Joyner

Printed in September 2012 in the United States of America by RR Donnelley & Sons in Harrisonburg, VA
10 9 8 7 6 5 4 3
Revised Edition

Library of Congress Cataloging-in-Publication Data

Bowen, Fred.
  On the line / written by Fred Bowen.
    p. cm.
  Summary: Worried that his inability to make free throws is making his junior high basketball team lose games, Marcus learns an unconventional underhand shooting method from a friendly custodian but is not sure he wants to use it. Includes a history chapter discussing great basketball players who have used the underhand toss.
  ISBN 978-1-56145-511-9 / 1-56145-511-3
  [1. Basketball--Fiction. 2. Self-confidence--Fiction.] I. Title.
  PZ7.B6724On 2009
  [Fic]--dc22
                              2009017028

For my mother, Catherine B. Bowen—
my first teacher and biggest fan

ONE

Marcus Devay leaped above the tangle of players stretching high for the rebound and snapped down the basketball. In one smooth motion, he took a quick dribble and sent a fadeaway jump shot toward the basket. The ball angled off the glass backboard and dropped cleanly through the net.

Marcus's teammates cheered as Marcus and the other Forestville Middle School Cardinals raced downcourt to play defense.

"All right, Marcus."

"Smooth move."

"You're the man, Marcus."

A satisfied smile creased Marcus's face as he got into position on defense. "Hands up," he called to his teammates as he waved his hands above his head. "Tough D."

A Bradley Hills guard tossed a long, off-center shot toward the basket. Marcus moved in for the rebound, jumped, and snagged the ball. He wrapped both hands around it, then zipped a bullet pass to his teammate Daniel Grady and dashed upcourt.

Daniel dribbled up the middle of the court, weaving his way past several players. At the last instant, he flipped a high pass to Marcus, who was sprinting toward the basket. Marcus took one final step and jumped. He caught the ball and, as he floated to the basket, laid a soft shot up and in. The basket stretched Forestville's lead to 50–44.

"Time out! Time out!" the Bradley Hills coach shouted from the sidelines.

The Forestville Cardinals were full of cheers and high fives as they gathered at the bench.

"Okay, cut the celebrations," Coach Lerner said. "We're only up by six points, and there are almost three minutes to go.

2

Plenty of time left. We've got to keep playing good defense and keep rebounding."

Coach Lerner looked around the circle of seventh- and eighth-grade boys. Then he stared straight at Marcus, the tallest of the group. "Let's try to get the ball in to Marcus. And Marcus, you've got to take it up strong. They may try to foul you."

Marcus nodded silently. *I hope I don't have to take any foul shots,* he thought. *I hate taking foul shots.*

"And remember," Coach Lerner continued, "we need good..."

"DEE-fense!" the team yelled. The players ran onto the court ready to play.

But Bradley Hills quickly cut the lead to four when its star forward got lucky with a desperate jump shot that bounced off the backboard, onto the rim, and through the net.

Marcus jogged upcourt, set up near the right side of the basket, and held up his left hand, signaling for the ball. Carl LaRue, a Forestville guard, saw that Marcus was open and fired a pass to him. Marcus tried to dribble around a Bradley Hills defender to the basket, but the defender gave him a swift shove. Marcus managed to balance on one foot long enough to send an awkward scoop shot to the hoop.

Phweeet! The referee's whistle shrieked as Marcus tumbled to the floor and the ball headed for the basket. It teetered on the rim for a few seconds, but fell off to the side. Marcus slammed his fist against the floor in frustration.

"Foul on blue, number 12," the referee called.

The referee signaled that Marcus would get two shots.

As Marcus slowly prepared to take his foul shots, all the game's action froze. Players stood motionless in their positions along the lane. The referee was still. The crowd was quiet. And all eyes were on Marcus.

Marcus spun the ball in his hands and bounced it low and hard three times. Each bounce made a loud *thump* on the gym floor. *Come on, you can do it,* Marcus thought to himself as he stared at the rim. *It's an easy shot, you've got to make it.* Then he took a deep breath, brought the ball up high, and flicked it toward the basket with a snap of his wrist. The ball clanged off the back of the rim, onto the floor, and back to Marcus. He pounded the ball against the floor with a short, angry bounce and then tossed it to the referee.

"Second shot," the referee said, holding up the ball. "Don't move until the ball touches the rim."

This time Marcus's shot was way short. It barely grazed the front edge of the rim. Marcus shut his eyes and hung his head for a brief moment before turning around and racing downcourt. *Still up by four,* Marcus thought as he ran. *We've gotta hang on.*

The Bradley Hills team worked the ball around the Forestville zone defense. A Bradley Hills forward slashed to the basket.

Tulane Hayes, a Forestville forward, reached in for the ball but grabbed the Bradley Hills shooter's arm.

Phweeet! "Foul," the referee called, pointing to Tulane. "Two shots, blue."

The Bradley Hills player calmly stepped to the line and sank both free throws. The lead melted to two points, 50–48, with thirty seconds to go.

Daniel Grady and Carl LaRue, the Forestville guards, played a desperate game of keep-away as the seconds ticked off the clock. Marcus moved out to take a pass.

The moment Marcus caught the ball, the Bradley Hills coach was off the bench and on his feet.

"Foul him!" he yelled, pointing to Marcus.

A pair of players pounced, slapping Marcus's arms.

Phweeet!

The Bradley Hills coach clapped as the referee called the foul.

"Number five on the arm," the referee said. Then, pointing to Marcus, he said, "Number three is shooting two."

"Time out!" the Bradley Hills coach shouted.

Marcus felt dazed as he walked slowly to the Forestville bench. He hardly listened to Coach Lerner giving instructions to the team. There were twelve seconds left on the clock and Forestville was only up by two points. Marcus looked past the huddle and stared at the Bradley Hills coach. *He wanted them to foul me,* Marcus thought, *because he thinks I'm going to miss the shots.*

As the teams moved back onto the court, Coach Lerner grabbed Marcus by the arm. "Use your legs and follow through," he reminded Marcus.

Daniel jogged up to his buddy as Marcus made his way to the line. "You're the man, Marcus," he said confidently.

But Marcus barely heard him. All he could hear was the pounding of his heart. It sounded like it was going to pound right through his chest and team jersey. *I've gotta make these shots,* Marcus kept saying to himself as he stepped to the line.

But the moment the first shot left Marcus's hand, it didn't feel right. The ball bounced off the rim and fell to the right.

"Second shot," the referee said as he handed the ball to Marcus. "Ball's live."

By now, Marcus could barely feel his hands and feet. He took a deep breath, puffed up his cheeks, and blew out a burst of air. He looked directly up at the basket and took his shot.

"Short!" he screamed as the ball started to fall. The ball thudded against the front rim, and the Bradley Hills center snatched the rebound.

"Back on defense!" Coach Lerner shouted, waving and motioning wildly from the sidelines. Marcus glanced at the clock as he raced downcourt, wishing the game were over.

The crowd started the final countdown as the Bradley Hills players looked frantically for the last shot. "Ten...nine...eight..."

A Bradley Hills guard dribbled toward the basket and Marcus moved over for the block. At the last moment, the guard fired a pass to a teammate standing past the three-point line.

"Four...three...two..."

The ball was in the air. Marcus stood helpless near the basket. He followed the flight of the ball with his eyes and knew. He knew that the shot was good and the game was lost.

He shut his eyes just before the ball splashed through the net.

8

TWO

Marcus didn't look up as he walked out of the winter cold and through his front door. He plopped his gym bag down on the living room floor with a thud. Then he slumped into a chair, twisted to the right, and hung his long legs over the arm.

"Is that you, Marcus?" his mother called from the family room.

"It's us," Marcus's father answered as he came inside and closed the front door.

"The high school principal made it to a game on a Monday?" Mrs. Devay said in astonishment.

"Yeah, luckily my meeting with the teachers got over early, so I walked down to the junior high," Mr. Devay replied. "I got there in time to see Marcus play." He glanced over at Marcus, but Marcus was staring straight ahead.

"Well, how did it go?" Marcus's mom asked as she entered the living room.

Marcus turned his head away from his mother.

"They lost a really close one," his dad said. "On a last-second basket."

"Oh, no. That's too bad," his mother said, looking at Marcus, who clearly was in no mood to talk. "How did Marcus do?" she asked, turning her attention to her husband.

"Oh, he did really well. He led the team with twenty-two points and must have had more than ten rebounds. He blocked some shots, but..."

"But what?" Mrs. Devay asked.

"But he missed a couple of foul shots at the end—"

"Four," Marcus said, interrupting.

"What?" Mrs. Devay looked over at Marcus, who finally met her eyes.

"I missed four straight foul shots in the

last minute to lose the game," Marcus said slowly, his anger growing as he remembered each missed shot.

"*You* didn't lose the game," his father protested. "You just missed a couple of shots at the end."

"Four," Marcus said again. Then he bolted out of the chair and paced around the room, swinging his long arms as he walked. "I can't believe I missed all those shots!" he moaned.

"Missed all what shots?" Marcus's older sister, Bree, asked as she breezed into the room.

"Marcus missed a couple of foul shots and his team lost by one point," Mr. Devay explained to his daughter.

"*Four*. I missed *four* foul shots, Dad," Marcus said.

"Four what?" Bree asked as she checked her hair in the mirror.

"Foul shots! Ever heard of them?" Marcus said. "I missed four foul shots in the last minute to blow the game."

"Doesn't sound like much fun," Bree said through a small smile.

Marcus rolled his eyes and turned on his heels. He walked back to the chair and flopped down into it.

"Come on. Stop feeling sorry for yourself," Bree said and then she started to sing. "Somewheeeeere oooover the rainbow...."

"Stop singing," Marcus said. He was tired of listening to all those songs from *The Wizard of Oz*. He knew Bree was going to be auditioning for her high school musical in a few weeks, but couldn't she just practice in her room?

"Marcus, you're upset about the game," his mother said. "You didn't lose it. Your team lost. And there's nothing you can do about it. Now come eat." She walked into the kitchen.

"Let's go, son," his dad said as he gently patted Marcus on the shoulder.

Marcus got up slowly. He took his place at the table as Bree placed plates around it, singing as she went. "Get over it," she sang in his ear as she plopped a plate in front of him.

"Lay off," Marcus said, pulling his plate

into position. "I'm not mad about losing the game," Marcus began to explain to his family. "It's just that I...you know...I..."

"You choked," Bree said flatly as she took her seat.

"Bree," her mom said with a sigh. "That is not helpful."

"I'm just saying that yes, he choked," Bree explained, looking back and forth between her parents but avoiding Marcus's gaze. "But it's no big deal. Everybody gets nervous."

Marcus shot an angry look at her.

"He thinks he's gotta to be the big star of every game," she said.

"At least I've *been* the star," he snapped at her.

"You watch. I'll get a big part in *The Wizard of Oz,*" Bree fired back.

"You two stop," his mother said firmly. "And Bree, try to be a little more sensitive."

"But Bree's right," Mr. Devay said.

Marcus looked up, surprised. Bree straightened up in her seat.

"Nobody makes every shot," Mr. Devay

13

said. "I remember a game I played in high school...."

Oh, no. Here we go, Marcus thought. He usually enjoyed his father's stories, but he wasn't in the mood tonight.

"I had to go to the line with about five seconds left. I needed to make two foul shots to tie the game." Mr. Devay took a sip of water and continued. "I made the first shot. But I was so nervous about the second shot that it barely touched the rim. We're talking air ball." He smiled at Marcus, but Marcus didn't smile back.

"At least you made one out of two," Marcus said. "If I had made half my foul shots, we would have won the game."

"Marcus, give yourself a break. You were just nervous," his father said. "Pass the green beans, please, Bree."

Bree reached for the dish. "Maybe Marcus just stinks at free throws," she said matter-of-factly to her father.

"Bree, you've said enough," her mother scolded. "Let's change the subject."

Marcus looked at his sister. His eyes

were blazing. Sometimes he couldn't stand her. He hated the way she was always singing those dumb songs from those dumb shows she kept trying out for—always worrying about how she looked. He hated the way she was always commenting on things she didn't know about.

But he really hated it when she was right.

THREE

Marcus stood in front of the mirror in the boys' locker room. His red Forestville practice shirt fell loosely about his waist and hips. His gray, baggy shorts reached almost to his knees. His white socks were pulled just over his ankles, the way he liked them.

"Come on, Marcus," Daniel said as he passed by on the way to the gym. "Staring in a mirror isn't going to help your game."

Marcus took one last look at himself and then walked with Daniel out of the locker room and into the gym. "We'd better be ready to run today," Marcus said as they stepped onto the gym floor. "Coach Lerner is going to practice us hard after losing to Bradley Hills."

Marcus was right. Coach Lerner put the Cardinals through their paces. Layup drills. Three-man full-court weaves. Wind sprints. The works.

In one fast-break drill, Marcus caught Daniel's eye as the two boys raced up the court. Daniel flipped a high pass over the defender's head toward Marcus, who was flying to the basket. The pass was behind Marcus, so the star center had to reach back, cradle the ball for an instant in midair, toss a shot toward the basket, and hope for the best. The ball banked high and soft off the backboard and dropped through the net.

The team burst into cheers.

"Wow!"

"That makes the highlight film."

"You're the man, Marcus!"

Coach Lerner was less impressed. "Daniel and Marcus are on defense now. Carl, Jamie, and Victor are on offense. Let's run it. This is supposed to be a fast-break drill."

Marcus pointed at Daniel and smiled as the two scrambled back on defense. Their teammates running the drill, Carl LaRue, Jamie Thomson, and Victor Ortiz, hustled downcourt looking for a score.

"Take Carl!" Marcus yelled at Daniel, pointing to the Cardinals starting point guard.

Just as Daniel lunged forward, Carl drilled a pass to Jamie, who drove hard to the basket. Marcus closed in on Jamie and forced him to pass.

Jamie bounced a low pass just past Marcus to Victor. Marcus whirled around, took one long stride, and leaped into the air. Victor was gliding toward the basket for what seemed to be an easy two points. But the ball had barely left Victor's hand when Marcus swatted it away with a thunderous block.

Again his teammates cheered.

"Take that!"

"Great block!"

Coach Lerner bounced the ball back into play. "Victor and Carl, back on defense!" he shouted. "Keep running, guys."

This time, Marcus hustled up the left side of the court. Daniel bounced him a perfect pass on the wing. Marcus took one quick dribble and went up for the shot. At the top of his jump, he flicked his wrist. The ball sailed straight to the basket.

Swish!

Phweeet! Coach Lerner's whistle stopped the action. The coach held a basketball over his head.

"Foul shots!" he called as he pointed to the baskets around the gym. "You know the drill. Break into groups of two. First player takes five shots, then the second player takes five shots."

Marcus motioned Daniel to a basket at the far end of the gym. The two boys walked in that direction as Coach Lerner continued to shout instructions.

"Keep track of how many you make. We have to make our free throws if we want to win our games."

Marcus winced at the coach's words as he walked toward the basket.

"You want to go first?" Daniel asked.

Marcus shook his head. "Nah, you go first," he said.

Daniel went to the line, set his feet apart, and casually tossed up a shot. *Swish*. It was good.

After five shots, the boys switched places.

"Four out of five," Marcus said to Daniel as he stepped to the line. "I hope I shoot that well."

Marcus spread his feet out and leaned over at the waist. He spun the ball in his hands and bounced the ball hard three times against the floor. As he stared at the basket, he had flashbacks of the Bradley Hills game and his missed foul shots, but he tried to shake them off. *Come on,* he said to himself, *it's the easiest shot in basketball.*

Marcus focused on the basket, dipped at the knees, and shot. The ball bounced off the front rim.

"A little higher," Daniel said.

Marcus pounded the ball even harder as he set up to shoot again. His second shot bounced against the back rim and popped over the front rim.

"How's it going?" Coach Lerner asked as he walked up to the two boys.

"Not so good," Marcus said, catching a bounce pass from Daniel. "I missed my first two foul shots."

Coach Lerner stood next to Marcus at the foul line. "When you're in a slump," he instructed, "you have to go back to your fundamentals."

Marcus stood with the basketball on his hip as the coach reviewed the basics of a good foul shot. "Spread your feet out so you feel comfortable and balanced," Coach Lerner said. "Keep the elbow of your shooting arm in toward your body when you shoot, bend your knees, and follow through."

Coach Lerner pantomimed a foul shot and then said, "Let's see you try it."

Marcus did just as his coach had instructed. He spread his feet, kept his elbow in, bent his knees, and followed through. But his shot spun around the rim and fell out.

Coach Lerner sighed and shrugged. "Your shot looks good," he said as he patted Marcus on the shoulder. "Don't worry, they'll start going in."

Marcus looked up at the rim again after Coach Lerner had walked away. The basket seemed farther than fifteen feet away. He shot again, and the ball sprang off the backboard and to the side. Another miss.

Marcus shook his head. "I don't think Coach is right," he said as Daniel passed him the ball. "Shots never look good when they don't go in."

FOUR

Marcus darted to the right wing and threw out his hands. "I'm open!" he yelled above the cheers of the after-school crowd.

Carl LaRue snapped Marcus a pass. Marcus dribbled hard to the basket and squeezed past two Stonegate defenders. As Marcus went up for the shot, he felt an elbow jab into his left side.

Phweeet! The whistled sounded just as Marcus released his shot. The ball bounced around the rim, teetered on the edge, and fell through the net.

"Yes! Yes!" Marcus shouted, pumping his fist in the air.

The referee chopped down with his hand,

signaling that the basket was good. "Foul on number ten in black, one shot."

"Great shot," Daniel said, clapping Marcus on the back. "We're up by six with three minutes to go. Make the foul shot, and we'll play good defense."

As Marcus stepped nervously to the foul line, he gave himself a silent pep talk. *Come on, you can do it. You've made a couple of foul shots today. Remember, keep your elbow in, bend your knees, and follow through.*

But the pep talk didn't work. His foul shot drifted off to the right. Stonegate rebounded and headed downcourt, looking to cut the Forestville lead.

"Forget the foul shot, Marcus," Coach Lerner called from the sidelines. "Play defense."

But Marcus was still thinking about his miss when a Stonegate forward canned a short jump shot. Stonegate was four points away from tying the game. Coach Lerner called time out.

The Cardinals ran off the court and quickly huddled around Coach Lerner. They were out of breath, but full of questions.

"Coach, should we stall?"

"How many time outs left?"

"Should we stay in zone on defense?"

Coach Lerner held up his hand to stop all the talk. "Okay," he said. "It's 46–42. We're up by four with two minutes to go. Don't stall. Keep looking for good shots. Stay with the zone defense and remember: block out and rebound."

Marcus stood silently on the edge of the huddle, nodding and nervously shifting his weight from one foot to the other. The game was too much like the Bradley Hills game. "I hope I don't have to go to the line again," he whispered to Daniel.

"You'll do okay," Daniel insisted.

The Cardinals followed Coach Lerner's instructions. They passed the ball smartly, moving quickly around the Stonegate defense.

Finally Jamie Thomson tossed up a short jumper that bounced high off the rim. Marcus jumped above the crush of players around the basket and tipped the ball back to Daniel. The Cardinals went back to passing the ball, looking for a good shot.

The clock started ticking away the last sixty seconds.

"Foul someone!" yelled the Stonegate coach.

Daniel slipped a pass to Marcus.

"Foul him!"

Before Marcus could pass, the Stonegate center charged in and smacked Marcus's wrist.

Phweeet!

After calling the foul, the referee looked over to the scorer's table. The official scorer held up two fingers.

"The shooter is shooting one and one," the scorer called.

"All right, Marcus," Coach Lerner shouted as he clapped his hands. "Be a shooter."

Marcus was a jumble of nerves. He carefully placed his feet just inches behind the foul line. *I've got to make the first shot to get a chance at the second,* he told himself. *Elbow in. Knees bent. Follow through.*

He kept his eyes on the basket, dipped, and flicked the ball as he came up on his toes. As soon as the ball was airborne, Marcus sensed that he had not followed through enough. "Short," he said under his breath.

Both teams moved in, looking for the rebound. But the ball bounced softly above the front rim, dangled in midair for a moment, and dropped straight through the net.

Marcus sighed with relief.

"All right, Marcus."

"Clutch free throw."

"You're the man."

Marcus missed the second shot, but it hardly mattered. A few seconds later, Stonegate threw up a reckless three-pointer and Marcus grabbed the rebound. He held the ball high above his head and looked for an open teammate.

"Someone foul him!" the Stonegate coach screamed.

"Marcus!" Daniel called, suddenly sprinting upcourt.

Before the Stonegate players could react, Marcus flipped a no-look pass up the court. Daniel dashed under the ball. Instead of heading for the basket, Daniel dribbled in zigzagging circles and let the clock tick down.

Marcus felt like laughing out loud as he watched the Stonegate players chasing after Daniel. They finally caught the Forestville guard and fouled him. Only twelve seconds were left on the clock—not enough time to change the outcome.

Forestville had won!

Minutes later, Marcus and Daniel sat laughing in front of their lockers. "That was a great move, running upcourt," Marcus said.

"I knew you'd get the rebound, big guy," Daniel said.

"I was just happy I didn't have to take any more foul shots," Marcus said, shaking his head. "Man, I hate foul shots."

"You made some today," Daniel protested.

"Not many."

Marcus spied Sam Lee-Hart, the team's manager, across the locker room with the score sheet under his arm.

"Hey, Sam," Marcus called, keeping his voice low. "Can we take a look at the score sheet?"

"You know the coach doesn't like guys looking at the stats," Sam said.

"Come on," Marcus insisted. "Coach isn't around. Just a quick look."

Sam looked around. "Okay, just a quick look," he said.

The two boys scrambled across the room to study the sheet.

		GAME SUMMARY									
		2 PT: F.G.		3 PT: F.G.		FREE THROW		RB	AST.	T-OV.	PF	TOT. PTS.
NO.	NAME OF PLAYER	ATT.	MADE	ATT.	MADE	ATT.	MADE					
	M. Devay	8	14	0	0	3	10	13	1	2	3	19
	D. Grady	1	3	1	2	1	0	2	5	3	2	5
	J. Thomson	1	4	0	0	2	3	3	1	1	2	4
	T. Hayes	4	10	0	1	3	5	6	2	3	3	11
	C. LaRue	2	6	0	1	4	4	2	1	1	0	8
	V. Ortiz	0	1	0	0	0	0	3	0	1	2	0

"See?" Marcus said, pointing at the sheet. "I was three for ten from the foul line. That isn't exactly lighting it up."

"So what?" Daniel argued. "You did about everything else. You had nineteen points, thirteen rebounds. You're still the man, Marcus."

"I'm not the man from the line."

"You just need some practice."

"I need something," Marcus said, still staring at the sheet and shaking his head.

FIVE

The next afternoon, Marcus knelt under the basketball hoop in the driveway next to Daniel's house. He pressed the end of a metal tape measure to the dark tarmac. As Marcus held down his end, Daniel pulled the other end away from the basket.

"Here's fifteen feet," Daniel called, holding the tape to the ground.

"Mark it with the chalk," Marcus said.

Daniel drew a white chalk line on the black driveway.

Marcus walked out to the line as he let the tape snap back into its roll. "That line's kinda crooked," he observed.

"It's good enough," Daniel said. "What do you want to play?"

"One on one." Marcus laughed. "You against me."

"Yeah, right. Like I can cover you. Come on, we're supposed to be practicing foul shots."

"Let me get warmed up," Marcus said as he dribbled in for a left-handed layup.

The two friends started moving around, talking as they sent jump shots into the Saturday afternoon sunshine.

"Have you started that local history project for Ms. Finch?" Daniel asked. He bounced a pass to Marcus.

"Not yet," Marcus said as he laid the ball in the basket. "But I've got a great topic."

"What are you gonna write about?"

"The high school had a championship team thirty years ago," Marcus explained, flipping a behind-the-back pass to Daniel. "I figure I can write a report on that."

"Cool."

"Yeah, all I've got to do is read the sports sections from the old papers at the library." Marcus swished an eighteen-foot jumper from the corner.

"Come on, Marcus," Daniel said. "You're just stalling. Let's practice your free throws."

"All right. All right." Marcus stepped to the chalk line and eyed the basket. "Are you sure this is fifteen feet?" he asked.

"Quit stalling. You helped me measure it!" Daniel said.

Marcus put the ball on his hip and was quiet for a minute. "You know, this driveway is kind of slanted," he said, looking around.

"Marcus! Shoot the ball!" Daniel shouted.

"Hey, guys, what's up?" Two Cardinals teammates, Carl LaRue and Tulane Hayes, stood at the end of the driveway.

"Trying to get the man to practice his free throws," Daniel called out to them, pointing at Marcus.

"Good idea," Carl teased.

"He needs it." Tulane laughed.

Marcus shot an annoyed look at Carl and Tulane. Marcus didn't mind Daniel teasing him; Daniel was his best buddy. But Carl and Tulane were different.

"You guys want to play two-on-two?" Marcus asked, moving away from the foul line.

"Sure. What are the teams?" asked Carl as he and Tulane walked up the driveway.

"You guys against us," said Marcus.

"You guys are taller," protested Tulane.

"We'll switch teams every five baskets," said Daniel.

"So what?" Tulane said. "Whoever plays with Marcus wins."

"Wait," said Carl. "Marcus, aren't you supposed to be practicing your free throws? Let's play Twenty-One."

Marcus groaned.

"Remember, you get two points for a foul shot and one point for a layup. The first one to twenty-one wins."

"Yeah, you shoot a foul shot and then a layup," Daniel said. "And if you make both shots, you get to take another two shots— another foul shot and another layup. If you miss one of the shots your turn's over."

"Right. If you miss your foul shot and make your layup, you get one point, but your turn's over," Carl added. "Oh, yeah. I almost forgot. You have to make your *very first* foul shot."

Marcus shook his head. "That's not real basketball. Let's play two-on-two."

"You're just afraid you won't win at Twenty-One," Tulane said.

"I am not," snapped Marcus. "You want to play Twenty-One? Fine. Who goes first?"

Carl tossed Marcus the ball.

"You," he said. The words sounded like a dare.

Marcus stood at the white chalk line as the other boys gathered near the basket. Marcus brought the ball up over his head and flicked it toward the hoop. The shot was long, and banged against the backboard and onto the driveway. Marcus grabbed the ball on the bounce and went up for the layup.

"One point," he said as the ball went through the net.

Carl shook his head. "Remember? You can't take a layup until you hit *your very first* foul shot. You've got to 'break the ice,'" Carl said with a wide smile. "You've got zero."

Marcus stood off to the side with his arms crossed over his chest and watched the other kids make their first foul shots and rack up points.

When Carl put in a layup after a missed foul shot, he tossed the ball to Marcus.

"Your turn," he said.

Marcus took his spot at the line. "What's everybody's score?" he asked.

"I've got seven," Daniel said.

"I've got seven, too." Carl smiled.

"Four," Tulane said, then added, "You've got zero, Marcus."

"I wasn't asking for *my* score," Marcus said sharply. Then he took his shot. Air ball. "This is stupid. Let's play some real basketball!"

"This is real basketball," Carl said. "Last time I checked, they gave points for free throws."

The game continued. The other boys' scores climbed higher, but Marcus's score stayed stubbornly at zero. He couldn't break the ice.

After Carl nailed the final shot for the win, Tulane said, "Let's play again."

"I've gotta go," Marcus said sourly. He picked up his ball from the grass. "It's getting dark."

"Come on, Marcus," Daniel begged. "We'll play a couple of quick games of two-on-two."

Marcus kept walking with his back to the boys. "Gotta go," he said without turning around.

Six

Marcus walked home slowly, with his basketball tucked under his arm. With each step he remembered a missed shot in the game of Twenty-One.

He paused in the pale yellow beam of the streetlight. He spread his feet along a crack in the sidewalk as if it were a foul line. He bounced the ball three times, paused, and took a deep breath that sent a puff of hot mist into the cold air. Then he dipped his knees, brought the ball slowly over his head as he lifted up on his toes, and pushed it straight up into the light.

Simplest shot in basketball, he thought as the ball spun in the light. *No one covering me. Same fifteen feet each time.* Marcus reached out and caught the ball before it hit the ground. *Why can't I make it?*

Down the street, the bells of St. Mary's Church tolled six times. *Man, I'm late,* Marcus thought as the gong of the last bell faded. He tucked the ball back under his arm and began to run. He ran along the wide sidewalks of his hometown, past the houses with windows bright from the lights inside. Marcus was happy to be moving, his long strides leaving behind the memory of his missed shots at Daniel's house.

Bree was singing when Marcus burst through the Devays' front door. "Follow the yellow brick road, follow the yellow brick road, follow follow follow follow—" When she saw Marcus, she stopped singing. "You're late, little brother," she said. "Mom was looking for you. And she's mad."

"Try not to look so happy," Marcus said.

"Marcus, is that you?" his mother's voice came from the kitchen.

"Yeah. Sorry I'm late," he called back.

"So am I," his mother said. "Set the table."

Bree flashed a fake smile at him. Marcus flashed one back. Then he rushed into the kitchen and started getting out the silverware.

"I've told you to get home before the streetlights come on, Marcus," his mother said sternly. "I don't like you running around in the dark."

"Sorry," he said. He knew from his mother's tone that she didn't want to hear any excuses.

Bree came into kitchen singing, "Lions and tigers and bears. Oh my!"

"Are you going to keep singing the whole night?" Marcus asked angrily.

"I've got to practice," she said. "Tryouts are coming up."

"What's the matter with Bree's singing?" their father asked, coming into the kitchen right behind Bree.

"Nothing. It's just that she does it all the time," said Marcus, plopping plates around the table.

"Is something bugging you, Marcus? Something other than your sister's singing?"

his father asked as everyone sat down at the table.

"No."

"Did basketball practice go okay?"

"We didn't have basketball practice. I went over to Daniel's house."

"Did you practice your foul shots?"

"Yeah," Marcus said in a discouraged tone.

"How did it go?" his father asked.

"Not so great. But I still think Bree shouldn't be singing all the time," Marcus said, trying to keep the focus off his foul shots.

"Marcus, forget about the singing. Tell me, what did you do over at Daniel's?"

Marcus reluctantly began to talk. "It was Daniel and two other guys from the team and me," he started. "We played Twenty-One—"

"Twenty-One!" his father said with a big smile. "I used to love that game. You get two points for a foul shot and one point for a layup. But you have to 'break the ice.'"

"What do you mean, 'break the ice'?" Bree asked.

"It means you have to make a foul shot before you can score any points," her father explained.

"Uh-oh. *That* sounds like a problem," Bree said, ignoring Marcus's glare.

Mr. Devay looked at Marcus. "How did you do?"

Marcus looked down at his meal. "I didn't even break the ice," he said.

"Sounds like you're still struggling at the line," his father said softly. "But don't give up. Keep working at it. I know you don't like Bree's singing, but you've got to admit she works hard at it and she's getting better all the time."

"I'll admit she works hard at it," Marcus said bitterly.

"I'm a whole lot better at singing than you are at foul shots," Bree shot back.

"I tried to practice at Daniel's," Marcus said, turning to his father and ignoring Bree. "But it's not the same as the gym. The driveway is slanted—"

"Practice in the park," his mother offered.

"Yeah, but the wind is blowing, it's cold, and the sun gets in your eyes. Really, it's not the same as the gym," Marcus tried to explain.

"So, practice in the gym," Bree said impatiently.

"I can't. The gym is used for practices after school."

"How about at night?" Bree asked.

Marcus looked at his parents as they traded glances across the table. His mother had a funny grin on her face. "You're the high school principal. Any chance you might be able to get Marcus into the school gym at night?" she asked Marcus's father.

Mr. Devay smiled. "I can ask Mr. Dunn, the custodian, to let you in."

"Really?" Marcus asked.

"Sure."

"Then you won't have any excuses," Bree said.

Marcus knew that she was right but he ignored her anyway.

"How much homework do you have tonight?" his mother asked him. "Have you started that local history project?"

"That's not due for a while," Marcus said quickly, then looked at his dad. "Are you being serious? You mean I can practice in the *high school* gym?"

His father nodded. "I'll talk to Mr. Dunn tomorrow. I don't think he'll mind. Maybe he could even help you out."

SEVEN

Rap, rap, rap, rap, rap. Mr. Devay knocked firmly on the back door of the high school gym. Marcus bounced on his feet to keep warm in the dark cold. He glanced over his shoulder to the empty school parking lot where his father's shiny black sedan stood next to a battered pickup truck.

Bree rubbed her arms to keep warm. Mr. Devay was going to walk home after a few minutes and she was going to drive Marcus home later.

"Does he know we're coming, Dad?" Bree asked as she rubbed her arms harder.

"I told him we'd be at the back door at eight o'clock."

Just then the door creaked open. Marcus squinted into the dim light, trying to make out the man in the doorway. He was a tall, thin figure. His long, angular neck stretched into the night, his bony fingers clutching the edge of the door.

"Hello, Mr. Dunn," Mr. Devay said. "Here we are. Thanks for meeting us.'"

Mr. Dunn opened the door wider and the Devays stepped into a dark corridor. It was bright at one end where the lights of the gym spilled out of a pair of opened doors.

"Come in, come in, Mr. Devay," Mr. Dunn said in a low, hoarse voice as they walked down the short hallway.

"I'm glad Dad is with us," Bree whispered to Marcus. "This guy seems kind of creepy." Marcus nodded as he eyed Mr. Dunn's short, straggly ponytail and frayed clothes.

Marcus entered the gym right behind Mr. Dunn. The stands were pushed against the wall and the gym seemed as vast as a canyon.

"This is my daughter Bree and my son Marcus," Mr. Devay said to Mr. Dunn. Marcus shook Mr. Dunn's rough hand.

"Oh, I know Bree." Mr. Dunn smiled. "I've seen her in the school musicals. You have a very fine voice. Very fine."

"Thank you," Bree said, flashing a wide smile.

Mr. Devay placed his hand on his son's shoulder. "Marcus is going to practice his foul shots because he's been having some trouble on the line."

Mr. Dunn scratched his chin whiskers, which were grayer than his sand-colored ponytail, and nodded as if he understood. Marcus nervously bounced his basketball. The sound thundered through the gym. He stopped quickly.

"So do you still play?" Mr. Devay asked Mr. Dunn.

"I still fool around with the game a little," Mr. Dunn said.

Mr. Devay nodded and tossed his daughter the car keys. "You kids be home by nine o'clock," he said. "Drive carefully, Bree."

"Okay, Dad."

After Mr. Devay left, Mr. Dunn said to Marcus, "You can shoot at any of the baskets you like."

Bree sat on the floor, opened a book, and began reading. Marcus tossed his sweatshirt on the floor by the door. Then he dribbled over to a basket. "I better get warmed up," he said to no one in particular. With that, Marcus began to move around, taking shot after shot, enjoying the sound of the basketball on the polished wood floor and having the court all to himself.

Finally Marcus stepped to the line. Bree glanced up from her reading. Mr. Dunn stopped sweeping. He leaned on the long handle of the wide broom to watch.

Marcus bounced the ball in the gym's silence, then in a single smooth motion, he flexed his knees, brought the ball up above his head, and let it go. The ball touched the edge of the rim, bounced along the side, and fell off. Marcus went after the ball and stepped back to the line.

Another shot. Another miss.

"Do you want me to rebound for you?" Bree called out.

"Sure." He paused. "But no singing. And no wisecracks."

"I promise," Bree said. As Marcus kept

shooting, she stood underneath the basket and rebounded.

Another miss...*swish*...around the rim and out...*swish*...short...long...around the rim and in...air ball.

"Not so good, huh," Bree said after a series of mostly misses.

"The ball feels funny," Marcus said, examining it in his hands. "Maybe it's low on air or something." Marcus looked over at Mr. Dunn. "Can I borrow a school ball?" he asked.

Mr. Dunn didn't say yes or no, he just walked over to the storeroom, reached inside, and brought out a basketball. After a few quick dribbles, he snapped a perfect bounce pass that skipped off the floor and right into Marcus's hands.

"Try that one," Mr. Dunn said. "And bend your knees a little more, you're not getting much push-off." He stood at the side of the court and watched Marcus's next shot. The ball bounced around the rim and fell in.

"Better," Mr. Dunn said and returned to his work.

After some more practice and many more misses, Bree looked at her watch and said, "Come on, Marcus, we better get going."

Marcus put in a final layup and headed for the door, feeling discouraged and defeated.

"Thanks, Mr. Dunn," he said. "We'll be back."

"Okay," Mr. Dunn said without looking up.

Marcus and Bree walked out into the hall. "That Mr. Dunn is kind of weird, isn't he?" Marcus observed.

"He's not so bad."

"You think he's okay because he likes your singing," Marcus said. "But did you notice his hair and clothes?" Marcus shook his head. "Man, he looks like he slept in those clothes."

Marcus had his hand on the door when he suddenly remembered something. "I forgot my sweatshirt," he said. He jogged down the hall to the gym and grabbed his sweatshirt from where it lay just inside the door. But then he waited a moment at the doorway and watched.

Mr. Dunn stood on the foul line at the far end of the gym. He held the ball in front of him with both hands below his waist. Slowly he dipped his knees, then raised both arms together, lifting the ball *under-hand*. The ball sailed in a perfect arc to the basket.

Swish.

"Weird," Marcus whispered as he turned to leave.

EIGHT

Marcus reached to snag a pass from Jamie Thomson. He glanced over his shoulder to the basket as the Westridge center leaned against Marcus's back with his right hand up, guarding against a shot.

Marcus quickly decided against taking the shot and passed the ball out to Daniel Grady.

Coach Lerner stood at the Forestville Cardinals bench, shouting instructions.

"Come on, Marcus. You've got to work for position. Keep moving."

Marcus glanced at the scoreboard as the Cardinals passed the ball around the Westridge defense.

We're up by eight, Marcus thought. *I don't want to blow another game by getting fouled and missing my free throws.* He kept passing the ball, afraid to take a shot.

Finally the Cardinals tossed up a long shot. Marcus dashed in for the rebound, but a Westridge forward grabbed it and started dribbling downcourt.

"Come on, let's work for a better shot!" Coach Lerner yelled. "Defense!"

A Westridge guard darted to the basket. Marcus leaped, reaching for the block. But at the last moment, the crafty guard twisted his body and forced Marcus to slam into him.

Phweeet!

"Foul. Number 3 in red, with the body," the referee called, pointing at Marcus. "Two shots."

The Cardinals huddled quickly on the court.

"Come on," Daniel said, looking around the group. "We've got to play defense and get some rebounds."

"Yeah," Jamie Thomson agreed. "And let's move it around for better shots."

While the Westridge guard calmly dropped in two free throws, Marcus leaned in, waiting for the rebound that never came. Westridge was catching up. The score was 47–41.

Daniel dribbled upcourt and held up two fingers to call a play. "Two!" he yelled.

Marcus popped out on the right wing. Daniel hit him with a pass. Marcus saw a path to the basket, but hesitated. *I don't want to get fouled driving to the basket. Maybe I can hit a jump shot,* he thought.

Marcus sent the shot to the basket, trying to hope it into the hoop. But the ball bounced off the rim and the Westridge team was off and running with the ball. A quick Westridge basket cut the lead to four and brought Coach Lerner to his feet.

"Time out! Time out!" he shouted.

The Forestville team huddled around their coach. His face was red and he almost spit out his words. "Come on! Start thinking out there! We've got take better shots! Marcus, get in closer or move the ball around."

Coach Lerner looked worried as he glanced at the scoreboard: 47–43.

"All right, we're only up by four points. We need a bucket," he said, looking around at the team. "Let's run the pick-and-roll play with Marcus and Daniel on the right side."

Coach Lerner knelt down on one knee and began to draw a play on his clipboard as the team leaned in and listened.

"Jamie, you pass to Daniel on the right. Marcus, set a pick for Daniel here," the coach explained, pointing to the board. "Remember, Marcus, just stand there and let Daniel dribble by so you block the guy covering him."

Coach Lerner pointed to Marcus and continued. "Spin to the basket after setting the pick and look for a pass from Daniel. Any questions?" Coach Lerner asked. The huddle was silent. The coach nodded. "All right. Let's go!"

Marcus and Daniel walked quickly out onto the court. "Take it up strong to the basket," Daniel reminded Marcus.

"Yeah, but if you've got the shot, take it," Marcus told his teammate in a voice just above a whisper.

Daniel looked at him puzzled.

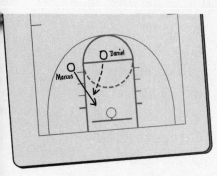

"Just take the shot if you've got it," Marcus repeated.

The Cardinals ran the play just as Coach Lerner had diagrammed it.

Jamie passed to Daniel on the right. Marcus slid out to set the pick. Daniel dribbled his man right into Marcus.

But just when Marcus was supposed to break for the basket, he hesitated. Daniel didn't know what to do. So he sent up a sloppy one-handed jump shot.

Marcus moved in for the rebound. But the ball hit the backboard and fell in. Marcus, relieved, flew down the court like he had wings.

"Great shot, Daniel," he called, pointing at his teammate and grinning. "You're the man!"

Daniel shot a quick glance back at Marcus. Daniel wasn't smiling.

The Cardinals hung on to the win. Marcus was all smiles as he walked off the floor, looking at the scoreboard. The numbers flashed the final score: 53–48.

After their showers, Marcus and Daniel stood side by side in front of their lockers. "Hey, what gives, Marcus?" Daniel whispered. "Why weren't you there for the pass?"

Marcus looked down, his big hands fiddling with the buttons on his shirt. "I don't know," he said, shaking his head. "I guess I didn't want to get fouled and have to shoot free throws."

"You should have told me that before we set up the play," Daniel said. "You let me down big time."

Marcus looked down at his feet and the floor.

"I thought you were practicing your foul shots up at the high school," Daniel said.

"I am, but I'm not getting any better," Marcus answered. He pushed his locker shut with his foot. Then he called across the locker room to Sam Lee-Hart. "Hey, Sam, how did I do from the line today?"

Sam looked down the columns in the scorebook. "Two for seven," he answered.

Marcus looked back at Daniel. "See what I mean?" he said.

"You've just got to keep practicing," Daniel said.

Marcus pulled his sweater over his head. "I don't know," he said. "Maybe I'll always stink at free throws."

NINE

"Hi, Mr. Dunn," Marcus said as the tall thin man pulled open the heavy metal door.

Mr. Dunn smiled. "You two come in quick," he said. "Your dad doesn't want me heating the outside."

Marcus and Bree stepped into the dark hallway. Marcus dribbled into the bright light of the gym and began to warm up, taking shots and darting around the floor. Bree read a book. Mr. Dunn went back to work, silently pushing the wide broom across the floor.

After a few minutes, Marcus stepped to the foul line. *This is it,* Marcus told himself. *If I don't get any better, I'm going to give up and stop all this nighttime practice stuff.*

Suddenly, the gym seemed different to Marcus. It didn't feel empty. It felt as though it were filled with people and all their eyes were fixed on him. Marcus bounced the ball three times. Each bounce seemed louder than the one before. He grabbed the ball firmly with both hands, took aim for the basket, and let the ball go.

The ball hit the front rim and bounced right back to Marcus.

"I stink at foul shots!" he shouted as he slammed the ball against the floor. The ball bounced in a high arc toward the basket.

Swish. Nothing but net.

Marcus's mouth fell open, and his sister laughed out loud. "Maybe you should shoot it that way," Bree teased as she got up and ran after the ball.

"Maybe so," Marcus growled. "I couldn't do much worse."

"Take it easy," Bree said as she tossed him the ball. "It's your first foul shot of the night."

Marcus could no longer hide his frustration. He hurled the ball wildly at the basket, smacking it over and over against the backboard. "First shot...second shot...third shot.... What does it matter!" he yelled. "I miss all of them!"

"If you're not going to practice your foul shots, we might as well go home!" Bree yelled right back.

Mr. Dunn put his broom aside and walked slowly toward Marcus. "Mind if I show you something?" he asked calmly.

Marcus looked Mr. Dunn up and down. The custodian stood just a few feet from Marcus with his hands out for the ball. His pants had a hole in the right knee and his blue work shirt was faded and the pocket was torn. His straggly hair was tucked behind his ears and hung limply on his shoulders. *What can this old guy show me?* Marcus thought.

"Come on," Mr. Dunn urged, motioning with his hands for the ball.

Marcus tossed him the ball. "Sure, go ahead," he said.

Mr. Dunn dribbled to the foul line and spread his feet along the line. He held the ball below his waist and in front of him.

He eyed the basket, then dipped slightly at the knees and sent an underhand shot spinning to the basket just as Marcus had seen him do on the night of his first practice. The ball floated over the front rim and through the net.

Swish.

"Why don't you try it that way?" Mr. Dunn suggested.

"Underhand?" Marcus blurted out.

"Sure, why not?" Mr. Dunn said. "You're big enough, strong enough. It should be an easy shot for you."

"Yeah...but...but...it's a girl's shot!" Marcus stammered.

"Hey, what's that supposed to mean?" Bree protested.

"Well, nobody shoots foul shots like that," Marcus said.

"Rick Barry did," Mr. Dunn said.

"Who's he?" Bree asked.

"Only one of the best players ever to play in the NBA," Mr. Dunn answered.

"He shot free throws underhand?" Marcus asked.

"Yup."

"Was he lousy at shooting regular foul shots or something?"

"No," Mr. Dunn said, shaking his head. "He was a really good shooter both ways. He just shot better from the line underhand."

"How did he do from the line?"

"About 90 percent—for his career."

"He made 90 percent of his foul shots?" Marcus said, unbelieving.

"Ninety percent," Mr. Dunn repeated, holding out the ball to Marcus. "Now, you want to give it a try?"

Marcus shook his head. "No way. I'd look stupid."

"I think it looks stupid for a player as good as you to be missing so many foul shots," Mr. Dunn said sharply.

Bree covered her mouth and tried to keep from laughing. Marcus stood silently, but he could feel his face burning with anger.

"How's this? I'll make a bet with you," Mr. Dunn offered. "If I make ten underhand foul shots in a row, will you at least try shooting underhand?"

"And if you miss?"

"I'll go back to my work," Mr. Dunn said.

Marcus thought for moment. "Okay," he said.

Marcus and Bree watched in amazement as the skinny, long-haired custodian sank ten straight underhand foul shots without even touching the rim.

"Ten," Mr. Dunn said matter-of-factly as the last shot slipped through the net. "Now it's your turn."

Marcus stood at the foul line. Mr. Dunn stood beside him. "All right. Get comfortable," he instructed. "Spread your feet out a little bit farther."

Marcus obeyed as Mr. Dunn continued. "Hold the ball on the sides, in your fingertips. Let your arms hang loose and relaxed in front of you."

Marcus held the ball just as Mr. Dunn had said. "Now, just dip your knees a bit and shoot the ball," Mr. Dunn instructed, making the underhand throwing motion.

Marcus dipped at the knees and flipped the ball toward the hoop. The ball bounced off the front rim. Bree grabbed the rebound.

"A little higher," Mr. Dunn said gently.

The next shot floated up and through the net. *Swish.*

Marcus kept shooting and a lot of his shots went in. The motion seemed simple and easy, almost effortless.

"Keep practicing," Mr. Dunn said after Marcus missed a few. "Just relax, trust the shot, and follow through."

Marcus nodded. More and more shots found their way into the basket.

Mr. Dunn smiled. "I think we may have ourselves another Rick Barry," he said to Bree.

"How does it feel, Marcus?" Bree asked.

Marcus smiled as another shot hit its mark. "The shot feels great," Marcus said. "But how does it look?"

"It looks pretty stupid," said Bree.

"Yeah, that's what I thought."

TEN

Marcus and Daniel ran up the steps of the town library and pushed open the heavy wooden door.

"We never should have left our local history projects until the last minute," Daniel said.

"You sound like my mom and dad," Marcus said as the two boys marched up to Mrs. Murphy, the librarian at the information desk.

"May I help you?" Mrs. Murphy smiled under a crown of gray hair.

"Yes, please. Where are the copies of the old town newspaper?" Marcus asked.

"The *Messenger*?"

"Yeah." Marcus nodded. "We've got to look some stuff up."

Mrs. Murphy turned in her chair and pointed. "There are computers in the reference room. Just click on 'Newspapers,' then *Messenger*. Then the years you want. Do you think you can figure it out?"

"I think so," Marcus said.

"I'd better show you," Mrs. Murphy said, getting up.

They walked to the reference room. Mrs. Murphy took the chair in front of one of the computers, and Marcus and Daniel each pulled up a chair next to her. With a couple of clicks of the mouse, Mrs. Murphy pulled up the *Messenger* file.

"Do you know the years you want?" she asked.

Marcus and Daniel nodded.

"Do the papers have the sports section?" Marcus asked.

"Yes." Mrs. Murphy smiled. "Are you boys doing your local history projects for school?"

"Yeah," Daniel said. "I'm doing mine on that big warehouse fire that took a whole day to bring under control. My mom told me about it. She remembers going out at night when she was little and seeing all those flames."

"That was the Hempstead Warehouse. They never did rebuild it," Mrs. Murphy said.

"And I'm doing mine on the town's championship high school basketball team from thirty-five years ago," Marcus said.

Mrs. Murphy nodded. "Oh, I remember that Einstein High School team. They were incredible." Mrs. Murphy pushed back her chair and headed for the information desk. "Well, the computer is all yours. You can search by year or subject. I'm sure you can handle that. Good luck, boys."

"Thanks."

Marcus moved over to the chair and computer Mrs. Murphy had used, and Daniel pulled in closer to the computer in front of him. "I didn't know you were doing your project on a warehouse fire," Marcus said.

"Yeah, a neighbor of mine, Mr. Petrocelli, was a fireman back then," Daniel said. "I'm going to interview him."

"That's a good idea. I don't know anybody

I can interview about the basketball team," Marcus said as he clicked some buttons on the computer.

The boys settled into pulling up the words and pictures of the past. Finally Daniel glanced over to Marcus and asked, "Was that Einstein team really any good?"

"Man, they were incredible!" Marcus exclaimed. "Take a look at this."

Daniel looked at the newspaper article Marcus had up on the screen. On the right-hand side was the team's season record.

"See? Einstein was undefeated in the regular season," Marcus said.

"Who did they play in the district championship?" Daniel asked.

"That's what I'm about to find out," Marcus said, scrolling down the page. "Wow. They played Bishop Fenwick in the first round and crushed them 73–48," he said. "This kid Ryan Robertson scored twenty-eight points!"

"Ryan Robertson isn't a kid anymore. He's probably older than our parents!" Daniel laughed.

HIGH SCHOOLS

Dream season for Einstein High

FROM STAFF REPORTS

The Einstein High School's boys' basketball team had a season to remember this year. Undefeated in the regular season, the team won two close games against rival Scarborough High School: 59-54, 67-63. They also hung tough in overtime to beat talented teams from Dunbar, 66-65, and Mayfield, 64-60.

Senior star forward Ryan Robertson was one key to Einstein's success. He led the team in scoring, with 282 points this season, and has been named to the state All-Star team.

"I look forward to the district championships," he said, "and I hope our physical play and rebounding will help us win."

—*Justin Brittain*

MORE BASK...
Top-rank
AA/A Rosw
McNair in a
squeaker i'
girls Ar
champion.
game. In
boys fin
Defen
led College
80-74 wi
Jean Jone
49 points
held Bro
forward
22 poi
below
T
Glenn
84 in
overt
edged
Academ
goals f
Davidson
Defe
led Colleg
80-74 w
Jean Jon
49 poin
held B
forwa
22 po
below h
To
Glenr
84 in

Einstein High School Season Scores		
DEC 8	at Latin	W 66-42
DEC 11	St Mary's	W 71-55
DEC 15	Austin Prep	W 72-37
DEC 18	at Dunbar	W 66-65 (OT)
JAN 5	Mayfield	W 57-51
JAN 8	at Valley Falls	W 60-50
JAN 12	at Wyngate	W 75-57
JAN 15	Kennedy	W 82-43
JAN 19	Chantilly	W 77-49
JAN 22	at Lafayette	W 44-41
JAN 26	Scarborough	W 59-54
JAN 29	at Mayfield	W 64-60 (OT)
FEB 2	Valley Falls	W 55-39
FEB 5	Wyngate	W 66-47
FEB 9	at Kennedy	W 80-45
FEB 12	at Chantilly	W 84-54
FEB 16	Lafayette	W 38-36
FEB 19	at Scarborough	W 67-63

"I guess you're right. Well, he was a kid back then," Marcus replied.

Marcus clicked a few more buttons and pulled up another issue of the *Messenger*. "They won their next game 61–53," he said, nudging Daniel with his elbow. "Let's see how they did in the finals. Wait. First let's see who was predicted to win." With a click of a button, Marcus pulled up an edition from a few days before the finals.

"Look at this! The team got a whole section of the newspaper!"

"Einstein played the Blair Blazers," said Daniel. "Did Blair have anybody good?"

"They must have. They only lost one game." Marcus scanned the list of Blair players. "Some guy named Dunn," Marcus said, "scored over twenty points a game."

"Sounds like he was the man," Daniel said, leaning in closer to the screen.

"Yeah," Marcus agreed. He looked over the screen and began to read out loud. "Einstein will have to find a way to stop Roderick 'Hot Rod' Dunn, the Blazers' high-scoring center. Hot Rod has scored over thirty points in each of his tournament games on the way to the finals."

"Come on," Daniel said, squeezing over to get in front of the computer. "Let's find out what happened. How did they lose with a guy like that on their team?"

"Maybe he was sick or hurt or something," Marcus said. He quickly went back to the keyboard and called up the newspaper page showing coverage of the final game. "Here it is," Marcus said as he read the headline: "Einstein Wins District Title, 66–65." He scrolled down the page.

"Look," Daniel said, pointing to a pair of pictures. "It says: 'The Thrill of Victory and the Agony of Defeat.'"

Marcus glanced at the pictures. In one, the new district champions celebrated, their arms up in the air and their faces lit up with pure joy. In the other picture, a thin, tired player with tears in his eyes sat staring blankly into the distance.

Daniel kept reading. "Star center Hot Rod Dunn thinks about the two last-second free throws that could have won it all!" He sighed. "Man, do I know how that feels."

Marcus studied the boy's long, lean face. It was younger, and his hair was darker and definitely shorter. But the set of the jaw, the look in the eye could not be mistaken.

"Daniel!" Marcus whispered, clutching his friend's arm.

"What?" Daniel said, trying to wrench his arm away. "What's your problem?"

"It's him," Marcus whispered, staring

wide-eyed and pointing to the picture on the screen.

"Who?"

"The weird-looking custodian at the high school. It's Mr. Dunn."

ELEVEN

Marcus burst through the front door with a notebook stuffed with paper tucked under his arm.

"Dad!" he shouted.

"Close the door behind you," his mother said.

Marcus hurriedly closed the door with his free hand. "Where's Dad?" he asked impatiently, catching his breath.

"Goodness, did you run all the way home?" his mother asked.

"Yeah, from the library. Where's Dad?"

"In the den, on the phone," his mother said. "How's the history project going?"

"Great! I got everything I need," he said, patting his notebook. "When's Dad going to be off the phone?"

"I don't know. He just got on," his mother said.

Marcus walked through the living room and slowly pushed open the door of the study. His father sat behind his large oak desk, talking on the phone and jotting down notes on a paper in front of him. When he saw Marcus, he motioned for him to come in and sit down. Marcus flopped into a big leather chair. He was still wearing his coat and scarf.

"All right, Mr. Szwed," his father said. "I'll talk to Zack's guidance counselor on Monday morning. Okay. Yes, that's right. I'll call you on Monday."

Mr. Devay hung up the phone with a sigh and tried to smile. He turned to Marcus and asked, "How did the research go?"

"Dad," Marcus said, bursting with excitement, "Mr. Dunn played ball!"

"I thought I told you that," Mr. Devay answered. His brow was wrinkled in thought, as though he were still thinking about his phone conversation.

"You asked him if he was still fooling

around with basketball or something. But Dad, he was a star!" Marcus practically shouted. "Hot Rod Dunn used to score twenty points a game, easy."

"Oh, he was a good player," Mr. Devay agreed. "He was tall, he could score, rebound—"

"Yeah, but did you know," Marcus interrupted, "that he missed the two foul shots that could have won the district championship for his team?"

"Yeah, I guess I remember something about that. I went to that game with your grandfather when I was about twelve years old."

Marcus yanked a loose paper from his notebook. "Look. I printed out the article about the championship game," Marcus said. He handed the paper to his dad.

Mr. Devay set his reading glasses on the end of his nose. He looked down and studied the article. "Yes, that's him," he said, tapping the newspaper picture.

"Check out the box score," Marcus said, handing his father another piece of paper.

BLAIR	FGM	FGA	FTM	FTA	RBS	PTS
Dunn	12	18	3	10	13	27
Connolly	1	3	2	2	3	4
Shube	3	7	3	4	4	9
Chatelain	6	15	4	4	2	16
Miller	3	5	1	2	3	7
Gura	0	0	2	2	6	2
Knapp	0	0	0	0	1	0
TOTALS	25	48	15	24	32	65

EINSTEIN	FGM	FGA	FTM	FTA	RBS	PTS
Fleming	4	8	4	5	7	12
Niparko	4	7	2	2	5	10
Dwyer	2	6	1	1	5	5
Robertson	7	16	6	6	4	20
Fisher	6	10	2	2	2	14
Cammariere	1	2	1	2	5	3
Pegula	1	5	0	0	1	2
TOTALS	25	54	16	18	29	66

"Mr. Dunn only made three out of ten free throws," Marcus said.

"Yeah, but he had twenty-seven points and thirteen rebounds," Mr. Devay noted.

"But even if he had made half of his free throws, his team would have won," Marcus said, shaking his head. "I can't believe he missed so many free throws. He never misses them now."

"Well, it's hard to make them in a game."

Marcus nodded. "Did Mr. Dunn shoot his free throws underhand back then?"

Mr. Devay took off his glasses, placed one of the earpieces in his mouth for a moment, and shook his head.

"No," he said. "Nobody shot underhand foul shots in high school. We called that a 'granny' shot."

"Mr. Dunn says that Rick Barry shot them underhand."

"Yeah, I guess he did, along with a few other pros," Mr. Devay said. "But I think that was a couple of years after the district championship game." He eyed his son. "Is Mr. Dunn teaching you the granny shot?"

Marcus nodded.

"How's it going?"

"Good. I'm getting really good at it."

"Have you tried it in team practice or in a game?"

Marcus shook his head.

"Why not?" his father asked.

"Because it would look stupid."

Mr. Devay tossed his head back and laughed. "That's the same reason the kids didn't shoot it that way when I was growing up. And I bet that's why Mr. Dunn didn't use it in the championship game."

Marcus stared down at the printout of the newspaper article. "I wonder why Mr. Dunn never told me anything about this," he mused.

"Well, he's teaching you the underhand shot, isn't he?"

"Yeah."

"Then in his own way he's telling you—he's telling you what he learned," his father said.

"What do you mean?" Marcus asked.

Mr. Devay tapped the picture of the much younger Mr. Dunn with his finger. "He's telling you not to worry about what other people think. And to go with the shot that gets the ball in the basket."

Marcus stared blankly at his father.

His dad sighed. "If Mr. Dunn had a chance to shoot those two free throws again, how do you think he'd shoot them?"

"Underhand, like he does now," Marcus answered without hesitation. "Just like Rick Barry."

"He can't play that game over again. But maybe he's hoping to keep another kid from having to relive memories like that," Mr. Devay said. He looked his son in the eye and smiled.

TWELVE

Come on, Cardinals!" Coach Lerner shouted during the practice scrimmage. "Let's see some hustle." The team raced downcourt.

Victor Ortiz banged a long jump shot high off the rim. Marcus leaped above the cluster of Cardinals to snatch the rebound. He drilled a quick pass to Daniel and took off up the right side of the court.

Daniel stopped dribbling just short of the foul line, but Marcus kept moving.

"I'm open!" Marcus shouted.

Daniel lofted a pass to the right. Marcus reached up, grabbed the ball, took one quick dribble, and hurtled the ball toward the hoop.

Victor moved in to block Marcus's shot but his hand missed the ball and the two boys collided.

Phweeet! Coach Lerner's whistle sounded as the ball dropped through the net.

"Yes!" Marcus yelled.

"And one," Coach Lerner called out, looking at Marcus. "Nice shot, Marcus. That's the way we take it to the hoop."

"Are we shooting foul shots this scrimmage?" Daniel asked.

Marcus quickly turned to Coach Lerner, waiting for an answer. *I'm going to try my underhand foul shot no matter how stupid it looks,* he thought.

"No. Keep running," he said, pointing to the baseline. "White ball, out of bounds."

Marcus and the rest of the red team hustled back on defense.

"What's the score?" Daniel called.

"Six to five, red lead," Coach Lerner answered. "Game to seven baskets."

"Come on, red!" Marcus yelled as he shifted around in the middle of the zone defense. "Hands up!"

The white team passed the ball carefully around the zone, knowing they needed a good shot to knot the score. The gym filled with shouts and the squeaks of sneakers against the floor.

"Switch men! Switch men!"

"Watch Carl, he's a shooter."

"Coming around back. Watch the baseline."

Carl faked a shot from the wing, fooling Daniel, who leaped up for the block. Carl flew by Daniel toward the basket.

"Pick him up!" Daniel shouted over his shoulder in a panic.

Marcus jumped up for the block as Carl tried to toss a running right-handed shot to the bucket.

Smack! Marcus swatted the ball with the palm of his hand, sending the ball bouncing to the sidelines. But just before the ball went out of bounds, Jamie Thomson, a red team guard, grabbed the ball and flipped it back into play.

Marcus leaped, snatched the ball, and flung a pass down the floor. The ball bounced once before Daniel gathered it in for the winning basket. The red team cheered.

"All right! Red rules!"

"Great hustle, Jamie."

"Heads-up pass, Marcus!"

Phweeet! Coach Lerner's whistle cut the celebration short.

"All right, break into pairs for free-throw practice," he called. "You know the drill. First guy gets five shots, then switch."

The coach held up a ball, adding, "If you make all five free throws today, you can shoot until you miss."

As usual, Marcus and Daniel headed to a basket together. "You want to go first?" Daniel asked.

"Nah," Marcus said. "You go first."

"Are you going to try out your new shot?" Daniel asked as he bounced the ball on the line.

"Yeah." Marcus nodded, looking nervously around the gym.

After the first group of players finished their foul shots, Coach Lerner pointed around the gym asking each player how many shots he made.

"Three...two...four...one...two," the answers came back.

"Come on, let's concentrate!" Coach Lerner shouted. "I want to hear some more fours and fives. Next group."

Marcus took his place on the foul line just as he had practiced so many times in the drafty high school gym with Mr. Dunn. He spread his feet comfortably apart, held the ball low in front of him, flexed his knees, and lobbed the ball up to the hoop.

Swish.

"What kind of dopey shot is that?" Carl asked, looking over from a nearby foul line.

"Yeah, did your grandmother teach you that?" jeered Tulane, who was standing near Carl.

"Why don't you worry about *your* game and I'll worry about *mine*," Marcus said. He could feel his face getting hot.

"He's one for one," Daniel noted.

"So am I," Carl said, as if to challenge Marcus. Carl turned toward his basket and resumed shooting his free throws.

Marcus turned to his basket too, but he paused before taking his next shot.

"You having second thoughts about your underhand shot?" Daniel asked quietly.

Marcus shrugged.

"Stick with it," Daniel said in a low voice.

"All the guys are going to laugh," Marcus said in a loud whisper.

"So what?" Daniel said. "Your shots are going to go in."

Daniel was right. One by one, each of Marcus's five shots found the bottom of the bucket. Only the last one touched the rim before it went in.

"How many did everybody get?" Coach Lerner asked.

"Three...three...four," the answers came back.

"Five!" Carl shouted.

"Five!" Marcus shouted even louder.

"All right." Coach Lerner smiled. "That's more like it." He pointed to the foul line where Marcus was standing. "Let's have a shoot-off," he said. "Marcus and Carl alternate shots. First player to make a shot when the other misses wins."

Marcus toed the line and eyed the basket.

He bounced the ball three times, then held it low in front of him. After a deep breath, Marcus dipped, lifted the ball up, and watched it splash through the net.

Out of the corner of his eye, he saw his teammates nudging each other. One of them smothered a laugh with his hand.

"Since when did you start shooting underhand?" Tulane asked from the circle of players.

"Since they started going in," Marcus said, pointing to the basket. Carl stepped to the line and confidently knocked another shot down.

"Six to six," Coach Lerner announced. "I don't know what you're doing, Marcus, but it's working. Okay, let's keep going."

The boys' shots kept falling. Seven... eight...nine...ten. The team cheered louder for every basket made.

Marcus dipped and shot his eleventh straight shot. Sensing it was short, he cried, "Get up there." The ball hung on the rim and obediently fell through the net.

Carl stepped up to the line again and

missed. He frowned, angry and frustrated. "Is Marcus's shot legal?" he asked, looking desperate.

"It's not only legal," Coach Lerner said, smiling. "It's good."

THIRTEEN

The Forestville Cardinals warmed up for the St. John's game by shooting jump shots in a large semicircle around the basket. Marcus stood at the foul line practicing his underhand free throws.

"How do you feel?" Daniel asked, standing beside him.

"Stupid." Marcus laughed as he lifted another underhand shot to the hoop.

Swish.

Daniel shrugged. "But they're going in," he said, motioning to the basket.

The buzzer sounded and the two teams gathered around their benches.

"Big game today, guys. St. John's is probably the best team we'll play this year," Coach Lerner said to the Cardinals.

Marcus fidgeted nervously. *I've got to play my best and stay out of foul trouble,* he thought, *and hit my free throws.*

"Marcus!" the coach said sharply. Marcus looked up, surprised. "Kenealy is a really good big man. You'll have your hands full covering him."

Marcus nodded.

"Okay, same starters. Marcus at center. Jamie and Tulane at forwards. Daniel and Carl at guards."

The two teams and their big centers took the floor and started right in on each other. After the teams traded several baskets and Kenealy picked up a quick foul, Marcus helped the Cardinals grab the lead by canning a tough fadeaway jumper. But St. John's came back as Kenealy sank a left-handed hook shot over Marcus's outstretched hand.

The score was tied, 10–10. His next trip upcourt, Marcus worked for position under the basket. He held up his left hand as he pushed Kenealy back with his right. "I'm open!" he shouted.

Carl slipped a bounce pass to Marcus. He got the ball, but Kenealy was all over him. Marcus faked to the right, then slid left and flipped up a crooked shot.

Phweeet! The referee looked at Kenealy and called, "Foul on number twenty-four. Two shots, red."

Marcus stood at the foul line and took a long, deep breath. *Relax, trust the shot, and follow through,* he told himself. He bounced the ball three times and lifted an underhand shot to the basket. The shot was perfect. The Cardinals pushed ahead, 11–10. His teammates were smiling—especially Daniel, who slapped hands with Marcus.

But Marcus noticed the St. John's players tucking their chins to their chests to hide their laughter.

Marcus ignored them and gathered himself for his second shot. This time, the ball bounced off the front rim.

Marcus raced back on defense. Kenealy ran by Marcus and shot a look at him. "Where'd you get that dorky shot?" he sneered.

Marcus didn't answer him.

St. John's grabbed back the lead, 12–11, with a long jump shot in the final seconds of the quarter.

Coach Lerner clutched Marcus's arm as the team came off the floor. "I'm going to put Victor in for you," he said, leaning close to Marcus. "I don't want you getting too tired. We're going to need you strong in the second half."

Marcus nodded and took a seat on the Cardinals bench. But he didn't stay seated long. Without their star center, the Cardinals quickly fell farther behind.

"Time out!" Coach Lerner popped up off the bench as another St. John's basket stretched the lead to 18–13. "Marcus, report in for Victor," he called as the team trudged to the sidelines with their heads hanging.

"Hey, Coach Lerner, what about a zone defense?" Jamie suggested.

"Okay," the coach said, looking around the circle of players. "Marcus, you take the middle of the zone. Come on, guys, we've got to come back."

With Marcus in the middle, the Cardinals began to crawl back. After a St. John's miss, Marcus and Kenealy both leaped for the rebound. Marcus got it, but Kenealy slapped at the ball in frustration as Marcus came down.

Phweeet! The referee blew his whistle and pointed at Kenealy. "Foul on twenty-four," he called. "On the arm."

Daniel pumped a fist into the air. "That's three fouls on the big guy!" he yelled.

"Is it a shooting foul?" Coach Lerner asked from the Cardinals bench.

Marcus quickly looked at the referee. *Oh, no. Am I going to have to take another foul shot?* he said to himself.

The referee waved his arms and shook his head. "Red ball," he said.

The buzzer sounded and Kenealy headed for the St. John's bench. His replacement entered the game.

With the St. John's star on the bench in foul trouble, it was the Cardinals' chance to catch fire. Tulane sank a quick jump shot. Daniel stole a pass and dribbled the length of the court for a twisting layup. Then the Cardinals pounded the ball inside to Marcus, who scored a pair of easy buckets on St. John's shorter substitute center.

The Cardinals had burst into the lead, 25–22.

As the final seconds of the first half ticked away, a St. John's guard drove to the hoop. Marcus leaped high, straining for the block. But the final shot floated over Marcus's hand and into the net.

The Cardinals were ahead by one point, 25–24, when the buzzer sounded at the half. Coach Lerner was on his feet, clapping loudly. Marcus wiped his face with a towel and drank water in thirsty gulps.

"Good half, guys. We're up by one," Coach Lerner said, still clapping. "Let's stay in the zone. It's working. Remember, move your feet on defense."

As the boys caught their breath the coach kept talking. "Carl and Daniel, drive to the basket every chance you get on offense. Remember, Kenealy's got three fouls. Two more fouls and he's out of the game."

Coach Lerner looked straight at Marcus. "Same goes for you," he said. "Take the ball up strong to the basket. Make Kenealy foul you." The coach smiled. "Maybe you'll get another chance to show off that crazy new foul shot of yours."

The team laughed as Marcus smiled weakly.

Practices are one thing, Marcus thought, *games are another. I'm not so sure I can make more foul shots under pressure.*

The Cardinals moved toward the court to warm up for the second half. Coach Lerner stepped out onto the court to make one last point. "Make sure you practice your foul shots! This is the kind of game we may win or lose on the line."

FOURTEEN

The five Forestville starters huddled at the center of the court just before the start of the second half.

"Come on, guys," Marcus implored. "We can beat them."

"Remember what Coach said," Daniel told the group. "Let's take it right to Kenealy. He's got to back off with three fouls."

But Kenealy did not back off. He blocked the Cardinals first shot and powered past Marcus for a pair of baskets.

One minute into the second half, the Cardinals were behind, 28–25.

Coach Lerner was on his feet as the team ran by. "Come on, Marcus, wake up!" he shouted. "Get your head in the game."

Carl LaRue faked a long shot and drove to the basket. As Kenealy stepped out for the block, Carl bounced a pass to Marcus under the basket. Marcus hesitated for an instant, checking over his shoulder for the St. John's center. As Marcus went up for the layup, Kenealy leaped and smacked the ball out of bounds.

"Red ball," the referee said as the buzzer sounded.

Marcus looked at the scorer's table and saw Victor trotting onto the court and pointing to him. Marcus walked to the bench, grabbed a towel, and took a seat.

Coach Lerner squatted right in front of Marcus like a baseball catcher. "You've got to take the ball up a lot stronger than that!" he said angrily.

"I slipped," Marcus said, looking down.

"You slipped?" The coach shook his head. "Sit and watch for a while," he said, walking away.

Marcus sat on the bench, staring straight ahead. He breathed slowly and deeply through his nose. He hardly saw the action on the court in front of him.

He looked down the bench at Coach Lerner. Marcus knew he hadn't slipped. He had hesitated because he was still afraid of being fouled, still afraid of shooting foul shots. After all, he had only made one out of two today.

Marcus slammed his towel onto the hardwood floor in front of the bench. *No more excuses,* Marcus scolded himself. *From now on, I'm going to play hard, take it up strong, and make Kenealy foul me if he wants to stop me.* Marcus's eyes narrowed with determination. *If I get fouled, I'll just shoot the foul shots. I've made eleven in a row at practice. I've even made fifteen in a row with Mr. Dunn.*

"Marcus!" Coach Lerner's voice interrupted Marcus's thoughts. In an instant, Marcus was beside his coach. "Go back in for Victor," Coach Lerner said, gripping his star center's arm. "We're down by three, 38–35. You've got to play hard. Take it right to Kenealy."

Marcus nodded silently and reported into the game. The first time up the floor, Marcus battled hard for position near the basket.

Daniel snapped a quick pass to Marcus, who faked left, then turned to the right for a short jump shot.

Swish.

Then Marcus grabbed the rebound off a St. John's miss and fired a pass to Jamie at the side of the court. Jamie lofted a perfect lead pass to Tulane, who was sprinting upcourt for a layup.

It was good! The Cardinals were back in the lead, 39–38!

After another St. John's miss and another rebound by Marcus, the Cardinals were back on offense. Jamie passed to Marcus on the right side of the hoop. This time, Marcus faked right and whirled left. Marcus and Kenealy collided as Marcus tried to squeeze up a shot.

Phweeet!

The two tall centers turned to the referee. "Foul on number twenty-four," the referee called, pointing at Kenealy. "Two shots."

Marcus stood at the line, staring at the rim. The referee handed him the ball.

Marcus's heart beat loud and fast.

Thumpa...thumpa...thumpa.... He could see the St. John's players rolling their eyes as he prepared for his underhand shot.

Marcus dipped and lifted up the ball. The ball bounced around the rim and fell in. Marcus's heartbeat slowed just a bit.

He dipped again. The second underhand shot felt perfect as it left his hands.

Swish.

The Cardinals were up by three points, 41–38. But their lead vanished as a St. John's guard nailed a long-distance three-pointer. 41–41. Tie score.

The teams traded baskets and the lead. Each time the Cardinals scored, St. John's answered with another bucket.

Racing upcourt, Marcus stole a look at the scoreboard.

Tie score with less than a minute to go, he thought.

The Cardinals worked the ball around the defense, searching for the winning shot. The St. John's defenders clutched and clawed the ball with every pass and dribble.

Marcus popped out to the foul line. "I'm open!" he screamed, holding out his hands for the ball.

Daniel tossed a pass, and Marcus pivoted to face the basket. Kenealy was right in front of him. Marcus faked to the left with a quick jab step, then drove to the right. He brought the ball up toward the basket with his right hand as Kenealy reached out for the block. The St. John's center slapped Marcus's wrist as Marcus flipped the ball toward the basket. The ball bounced off the backboard and away from the basket.

Phweeet!

All heads turned to the referee. "Foul on number twenty-four," he called out. "Two shots!"

Kenealy threw his head back as if he were in pain. "No!" he shouted and then trudged to the St. John's bench. It was his fifth foul. He was out of the game.

Once again, Marcus stepped to the line. *I've got to make both to clinch the game,* Marcus thought to himself. He dipped and softly lobbed the ball. Short. The ball fell off the front of the rim.

Standing on the line, Marcus could feel his teammates holding their breath as he leaned over and bounced the ball three times. *Easiest shot in basketball,* he reminded himself as he stared at the rim. Marcus took a deep breath, dipped, and lifted the ball up. The ball floated to the basket.

Swish! The Cardinals led 50–49.

St. John's scrambled downcourt. The final seconds ticked away. Twelve…eleven…ten… nine…. A long shot by St John's bounced high off the rim. Marcus stretched up to grab the rebound.

"Foul him!" the St. John's coach shouted, pointing wildly at Marcus.

A gang of hands slapped the ball and across Marcus's arms.

Phweeet! "Foul on green, number twelve. Red team is shooting one and one."

"Time out!" the St. John's coach yelled. The teams gathered around their benches.

Marcus was so lost in his own thoughts, he could barely listen to Coach Lerner's final instructions. *It's all so simple,* he told himself. *Eight seconds to go, up by one point. I'm shooting one and one. I have to make the first foul shot to have a chance at the second. And I have to make both shots to make sure we won't lose. Fifteen feet, nobody guarding me. The simplest shot in basketball.*

Marcus could feel every eye in the gym on him as he stepped to the line. *You can do this,* he told himself. *Trust the shot.* He eyed the basket, then bounced the ball three times, took a deep breath, bent his knees, and lifted up the ball.

Swish.

His second underhand shot was just as good. Just as good as the countless stupid-looking shots he had practiced with Mr. Dunn all winter. Just as good as the eleven in a row he had made to beat Carl in practice. Just as good as any foul shot Rick Barry ever made.

And as Marcus ran downcourt and watched a final St. John's shot fall far short of the basket, he knew. Marcus shouted to the rafters and threw his fist into the air, because he knew.

He knew he had come through.

FIFTEEN

The door swung open. "Hey, Mr. Dunn." Mr. Dunn peered out at the clear, starlit night.

"It's getting warmer," he said to Marcus and Bree. "Pretty soon you'll be practicing outdoors."

"You mean I can't practice here anymore?" Marcus asked.

"I didn't say that," Mr. Dunn said. "Come in."

Marcus and Bree followed him down the dark corridor and into the light of the gym. Mr. Dunn walked over to a machine in the middle of the floor. "You'll have to shoot at the basket down there," he said, pointing to the end of the gym. "I'm polishing the floor for tomorrow night's game."

Mr. Dunn flicked a switch on the machine, and the large round disc at the bottom began to spin. Mr. Dunn danced the whirring machine in small circles around the floor.

"I read about your championship game against Einstein!" Marcus shouted above the noise as he passed Mr. Dunn.

The custodian flicked the switch and the machine spun slowly to a stop. He looked at Marcus with narrowed eyes. "Where'd you read about that game?" he asked.

"At the library, on the computer. They've got all the old papers," Marcus said. "You were Hot Rod Dunn, a big star."

A small smile flickered at the edges of Mr. Dunn's mouth. "Not big enough," he said.

"My dad said you didn't shoot your foul shots underhand," Marcus said. "Did you know about the shot then?"

"Yeah, sure." Mr. Dunn nodded.

Marcus paused for a moment. "Why didn't you shoot them underhand, then?" he asked.

"I was too worried that it would look stupid," Mr. Dunn said, shaking his head.

"I know what you mean," Marcus replied. "I shot my foul shots underhand in the St. John's game," he said.

"Really?" Mr. Dunn brightened. "How'd you do?"

"I made the last three foul shots to win the game," Marcus said proudly.

Mr. Dunn nodded and smiled.

"Come on, are you gonna shoot or talk?" Bree called from across the floor.

"Hey, do you want to play a game of Twenty-One?" Marcus asked.

Mr. Dunn smiled again. "Do you think you can beat me?" he asked.

"I did pretty well against St. John's," Marcus replied.

"Okay."

The two walked over to the foul line. "Do you want to go first?" Marcus asked.

"Nah, you go first."

"I'll rebound, okay?" Bree suggested as she stood up.

"Okay, but no singing," Marcus said.

Marcus stepped to the line and looked up at the basket: fifteen feet away, but somehow it didn't seem as far as before. He dipped and lifted the ball.

Swish.

He went in for the layup and made that too. Four more foul shots and layups followed. Finally, Marcus's sixth foul shot slid off the rim and out.

"Sixteen points," Marcus said after tossing in a layup.

"Your shot looks good," Mr. Dunn said as he bounced the ball on the foul line.

"Every shot looks good when it goes in." Marcus smiled.

Mr. Dunn began to shoot. He reached twenty-one points easily but kept going. Marcus stood to the side, watching.

And somehow nothing looked weird to him anymore. Not Mr. Dunn's long hair. Not his tattered clothes. And not his funny-looking underhand toss that slipped cleanly through the net every time.

THE END

FREE THROWS
THE REAL STORY

Over the years, the game of basketball has changed. Today's players are bigger, and more of them are girls. They jump higher and run faster. Slam dunks have taken the place of two-handed set shots.

But one part of basketball has not changed: the free throw. The foul line is still fifteen feet from the basket. Nobody guards the shooter. Free throws still can make the difference between winning or losing a game.

Rick Barry was a great player and one of basketball's greatest free-throw shooters. Barry was a twelve-time All Star. In 1996, he was named one of the fifty greatest players ever to play in the NBA (National Basketball

Association). And Barry is the only player in the history of basketball to have been the top scorer in the NCAA (National Collegiate Athletic Association), NBA, and ABA (American Basketball Association, a pro basketball league that existed from 1968 to 1976).

Barry did a lot of his scoring from the free-throw line. During his *Rick Barry, who made ninety* ten years in the NBA, *percent of his foul shots, pre-* he was the best free-*pares for his famous under-* throw shooter for six *hand free throw.*

Rick Barry, who made ninety percent of his foul shots, prepares for his famous underhand free throw.

throw shooter for six years and the second-best free-throw shooter for four years. Barry made 90 percent of his free throws. That means that of every ten shots he took, he only missed one!

But the most amazing thing about Rick Barry is that he shot his free throws underhand. Barry did not seem to care how he looked when he took his foul shots. He just cared about getting the ball in.

"Players don't shoot underhand because it's not a macho thing," Barry once said. He said that guys should quit worrying about looking macho and just concentrate on getting the ball in the basket.

Another guy who didn't worry about how he looked on the foul line was Dave Gambee. He was a rugged, rebounding forward who played for several teams in his ten-year NBA career. He had a weird-looking foul shot: he would bend low, stretch one leg forward, pointing his toe like a ballerina, then toss the ball up underhand in a reverse spin.

Forward Dave Gambee, number 44, drives past San Diego players to the hoop.

And it worked! Gambee sank more than 82 percent of his free throws.

Other players, like Wilt Chamberlain, tried the underhand shot. Chamberlain was one of basketball's all-time greats. He was an unstoppable scorer and an awesome rebounder. But when it came to free throws, he was terrible. Chamberlain tried many different ways of shooting them, including underhand. The underhand shot worked better than most of Chamberlain's other shots. But the seven-foot-three, three-hundred-pound giant didn't like the shot. "I feel silly," Chamberlain said. Chamberlain, it seems, never learned the lesson that Rick Barry and Marcus learned: Sometimes looks aren't as important as getting the job done.

ACKNOWLEDGMENTS

A lot of the information about free throw shooting comes from an April 13, 1998 *Sports Illustrated* article, "Everything You Always Wanted to Know About Free Throws (But Were Afraid To Ask Shaq)," by Michael Bamberger.

Much of the information about Rick Barry was obtained from The National Basketball Association website, *www.nba.com*.

The author wishes to thank Jack Lewis of Silver Spring, Maryland, for his help with the *X*s and *O*s.

ABOUT THE AUTHOR

One of the biggest disap-
pointments of Fred Bowen's
life was that he did not make
his high school varsity basketball team in Marblehead,
Massachusetts. But he did not
stop playing. Mr. Bowen
played pickup basketball and
in recreational leagues for
twenty-five years. He played
on the same team, the Court

Jesters, for eighteen straight seasons.

Over a period of thirteen years, Mr. Bowen
coached thirty-one different kids' sports teams in
soccer, baseball, softball, and basketball.

Mr. Bowen is the author of a number of sports
novels for young readers. He lives in Silver
Spring, Maryland, with his wife Peggy Jackson.
His daughter is a college student and his son is a
college baseball coach.

Mr. Bowen writes a weekly sports column for
kids in the *Washington Post*.

Visit his website at *www.fredbowen.com*.

HEY, SPORTS FANS!

Don't miss these action-packed books by Fred Bowen...

Real Hoops
PB: $5.95 / 978-1-56145-566-9 / 1-56145-566-0
Hud can run, pass, and shoot at top speed. But he's not much of a team player. Can Ben convince Hud to leave his dazzling—but one-man—style back on the asphalt?

Quarterback Season
PB: $5.95 / 978-1-56145-594-2 / 1-56145-594-6
Matt expects to be the starting quarterback. But after a few practices watching Devro, a talented seventh grader, he's starting to get nervous. To make matters worse, his English teacher is on his case about a new class assignment: a journal.

Go for the Goal!
PB: $5.95 / 978-1-56145-632-1 / 1-56145-632-2
Josh and his talented travel league soccer teammates are having trouble coming together as a successful team—until he convinces them to try team-building exercises.

Perfect Game
PB: $5.95 / 978-1-56145-594-2 / 1-56145-594-6
Isaac is a perfectionist. This extends to everything in his life, but especially his love for baseball. He dreams of pitching a perfect game—18 batters, all out—and of earning a spot on the summer travel team. But Isaac hasn't learned how to handle it when things go wrong. After his latest meltdown, his coach asks him to help out with a Unified soccer team developmentally challenged kids and mainstream kids, all playing together.

Check out **www.SportsStorySeries.com** for more info.

Want more?

All-St★r Sports Story
Series

T. J.'s Secret Pitch
PB: $5.95 / 978-1-56145-504-1 / 1-56145-504-0

T. J.'s pitches just don't pack the power to strike out the batters, but the story of 1940s baseball hero Rip Sewell and his legendary eephus pitch may help him find a solution.

The Golden Glove
PB: $5.95 / 978-1-56145-505-8 / 1-56145-505-9

Without his lucky glove, Jamie doesn't believe in his ability to lead his baseball team to victory. How will he learn that faith in oneself is the most important equipment for any game?

The Kid Coach
PB: $5.95 / 978-1-56145-506-5 / 1-56145-506-7

Scott and his teammates can't find an adult to coach their team, so they must find a leader among themselves.

Playoff Dreams
PB: $5.95 / 978-1-56145-507-2 / 1-56145-507-5

Brendan is one of the best players in the league, but no matter how hard he tries, he can't make his team win.

Winners Take All
PB: $5.95 / 978-1-56145-512-6 / 1-56145-512-1

Kyle makes a poor decision to cheat in a big game. Someone discovers the truth and threatens to reveal it. What can Kyle do now?

All-Star Sports Story Series

Full Court Fever
PB: $5.95 / 978-1-56145-508-9 / 1-56145-508-3

The Falcons have the skill but not the height to win their games. Will the full-court zone press be the solution to their problem?

Off the Rim
PB: $5.95 / 978-1-56145-509-6 / 1-56145-509-1

Hoping to be more than a benchwarmer, Chris learns that defense is just as important as offense.

The Final Cut
PB: $5.95 / 978-1-56145-510-2 / 1-56145-510-5

Four friends realize that they may not all make the team and that the tryouts are a test—not only of their athletic skills, but of their friendship as well.

On the Line
PB: $5.95 / 978-1-56145-511-9 / 1-56145-511-3

Marcus is the highest scorer and the best rebounder, but he's not so great at free throws—until the school custodian helps him overcome his fear of failure.

Check out **www.SportsStorySeries.com** for more info.